CONTENTS

Adapted from stories by
Hans Christian Andersen, Charles Perrault
and the Countess Segur.
Translated from the French and re-told by
LILY OVEN.

Illustrations Copyright © MCMLXXX by Lito Publishers
English text Copyright © MCMLXXX by Brown Watson (Leicester) Ltd
Published in Great Britain by Brown Watson (Leicester) Ltd.,
55a London Road, Leicester LE2 OPE.
All rights reserved throughout the world.
ISBN 0 7097 0142 X
Printed in Czechoslovakia
50201/51/05

MY TREASURY OF

FAIRY TALES

Brown Watson
(Leicester) Ltd

Tom Thumb

THERE was once a woodcutter and his wife who were very poor. They had seven children, all boys, and none of them was old enough to earn his living. The youngest was only seven, and he was extremely small and delicate – in fact, when he was born, he was only as large as a thumb, and they called him Tom Thumb. He hardly ever talked. But he was very bright and clever, and if he didn't talk, he listened a lot. There was very little he didn't hear.

There came a very hard year, and there was great famine everywhere, and at last the woodcutter and his family had nothing to eat. And one evening when the children were in bed, the father said to his wife:

"We can no longer feed our children, and I can't bear to see them starve. Tomorrow we shall take them into the forest, and while they are collecting wood, we shall go away without them seeing us."

This was such a terrible thing that the mother would not think of it. But alas, what could they do? They had no food and no money to buy any. She began crying and sobbing, but at last he persuaded her, and they both went to bed in tears.

But little Tom Thumb was not in bed, as everyone thought he was. He was playing in a corner behind a cupboard, and he heard every word of this.

He crept back to bed, but lay awake all night, thinking about what he had heard. And the next morning he got up very early and went out to the stream, where he filled his pockets with small white stones. Then he returned to the house.

A little later they all set off for the forest. Tom Thumb told no one of what he had heard.

They soon reached the forest and went deeper and deeper, further and further, into it. Then the woodcutter began to cut branches from the trees, and his children tied them up in bundles.

When they were all quite busy, the parents crept away from them, and went home by a different path.

When the children realised they were lost, they began to cry. But Tom Thumb knew quite well how to get home.

Because as they had been coming along, he had dropped his little white stones all along the path. So now he told them to cheer up and stop crying and follow him.

They did this, and Tom Thumb simply followed the trail of little white stones, and led them back home.

But before they went to the house, they saw their parents in the yard, stacking the wood, and hid themselves, to hear what their parents were saying.

And they were still very unhappy, because when they arrived home, the lord of the manor was waiting for them to pay some money he owed them.

"We need not have left our children, you see!" sobbed the

9

mother. "With this money we can buy food. You are a cruel man!"

The poor woodcutter didn't know what to say, but he felt like a monster.

"It was you who thought of it!" she went on. "I knew all the time we should be sorry. Oh, my poor children! Where are they now? What are they doing? Supposing the wolves have got them?"

"We are here, mother, we are here!" shouted the boys, and rushed up to their parents, who hugged them and kissed them and wept over them.

"Oh, how happy we are! How happy!" the parents kept saying. "Are you very hungry? Yes, of course you are. Let us go and eat."

So they went into the house and the mother made a splendid

meal for them, and they were all very happy.

The boys told the parents how frightened they had been, and how clever Tom Thumb had brought them home. And the parents told the boys about the money they had received.

And they all stayed happy – till the money was all spent. Then it all started again. Hardly any food they had, and the parents unhappy and cross-tempered. And this time Tom Thumb guessed what the parents were thinking, and knew they were planning to take the children out again and lose them. And when the father said that tomorrow they would go out to cut wood, he knew he was right.

So again he got up very early in the morning, to creep out and fill his pockets with stones. But when he came to the door, he found it locked and bolted. He couldn't get out!

That afternoon, before they set out, the mother gave each of the boys a piece of bread. Tom Thumb decided to use his bread instead of the little white stones, and dropped it in crumbs all along the path.

The parents took them into a different part of the forest, even deeper and thicker than before. Then, while they were not looking, they slipped away from them.

Tom was not very worried, thinking he could again find his way back. But he had forgotten the birds. They had eaten every one of his crumbs!

Now they were indeed lost. The poor children were terrified, and ran this way and that, but found no way out.

Then at last Tom Thumb had another idea. He climbed to the top of the highest tree they could find, right to the very top, where he could see in every direction. And at last he saw, far away – a light! He hurried down from the tree, told his brothers, and began to lead them towards the light.

And after a while they came to a large mansion, and knocked at the door.

A woman answered the door. She seemed most surprised to see them, but she looked kind. So they told her they were lost, and very hungry, and asked if she could give them food and shelter for the night.

"Oh, you poor children!" she said. "Don't you know that this is the home of an ogre who eats young children? How can I let you stay here?"

But Tom pleaded with her. "But if we stay in the forest the wolves will surely eat us, but if we stay here perhaps the ogre will have pity on us and not eat us."

At last she let them in, thinking perhaps she could hide them away from her husband. She took them into the kitchen to get warm before the fire, and gave them some food.

They were just feeling comfortable when there came a great hammering on the door. The ogre had come home! Terrified, his wife rushed the children away and hid them under her bed, then went to let her husband in.

He asked if supper was ready and if the wine had been brought up. Then he sat down at the table.

Suddenly he growled: "I can smell fresh meat, wife!"

"No, no. It's the mutton that I'm cooking," she said.

But he went round the house sniffing, till he came to the bedroom, and there he found the children.

"Ha!" he roared. "Trying to deceive me, were you? Well, they'll make a fine feast for to-morrow night!"

"It just so happens," he went on. "That I have invited three ogre friends to supper to-morrow. This is splendid. Come out, all of you!"

They pleaded with him on their knees to spare them, but he was the cruellest of all the ogres. There was no kindness in him.

He went and fetched a long sharp knife, and went towards them, testing the blade. But his wife said:

"But why do you have to kill them now? There will be time for that to-morrow, and there's already plenty to eat – a young calf, two sheep and half a pig."

"You are quite right, wife," he said. "Look after these for to-night, then. Give them a good meal and get them to bed."

His wife was pleased with this, and gave the children more food, though this time they could eat very little, they were so afraid. Then she took them off to bed, in the room where her seven daughters were sleeping in one great bed.

They were ugly, cruel girls, like their father, and even in bed each of them wore a golden crown.

In the same room was another huge bed, and here the woman put the boys to sleep.

But Tom Thumb could not rest. He did not trust the ogre, and after a while he got up, took the golden crowns off the girls' heads and put them on his brothers. Then he put their woollen caps on the girls' heads.

Sure enough, during the night the ogre woke and began thinking about the boys. He got up, fetched his knife and crept into the room where they were sleeping.

He felt around and came to a bed. He put out his hand and touched a head – and there was a crown on it! So he went to the other bed, touched a head that was wearing a woollen cap – and believing these were the boys, he killed all his seven daughters. Then he went back to bed.

Tom Thumb was awake and very afraid. He lay there and waited till he heard the ogre snoring, then he woke his brothers, told them what had happened and bade them dress quickly.

Then they all jumped out of the window and ran off as fast as possible.

And for the rest of that night they just ran, and ran, not knowing where they were going, just glad to be alive, trying to get as far away from the ogre's mansion as possible.

The next morning the ogre was in a very good temper, which surprised his wife, for he was usually very cross. He said to her: "Wake those boys and tell them to dress and bring them down here."

But when she went to the bedroom and found her seven daughters lying dead, and the boys nowhere to be seen, she gave a great cry and fainted. Hearing this, the ogre ran to the room, and when he saw his daughters, he roared wildly.

"Oh, what have I done?' he shouted. "I will find those boys! I'll make them pay for this!"

He threw some water over his wife, and when she had recovered from her faint, he shouted:

"Bring me my seven-league boots! I'm going after them!"

His seven-league boots were magic ones, so that with each step he took, he covered more than seven miles.

His poor trembling wife brought him his boots, and helped him to put them on, and off he went after the boys, slamming the door behind him so hard that the whole house shook.

Across the countryside he strode, this way and that way, and it wasn't very long before he saw the path the poor boys had taken.

They were still running, and in fact not very far from their parents' house. But then in the distance they saw the ogre, striding from mountain to mountain, stepping over rivers as though they were little streams. He was so big!

Suddenly Tom Thumb spied a large rock with a narrow split down it. He told his brothers to squeeze into there and hope that the ogre would not find them. He himself kept watch behind a dandelion to see what the ogre was doing.

The ogre knew they were somewhere about, but could not find them. He was tired, too, and thought he might as well have a rest, for the boys were sure to appear soon. So he sat down .... against the very rock where the boys were hidden!

He only meant to rest, but he was so weary after all that running, and so angry about the terrible thing he had done to his daughters, that presently he fell asleep. He snored so loudly that the children trembled again, thinking perhaps he had his knife with him. But Tom told his brothers to creep off and run home quickly.

Then he crept out silently,

up to the sleeping ogre, and very gently pulled off the magic, seven-league boots, which he put on himself.

Being magic boots, they fitted anyone who wore them, so off he went, straight back to the ogre's mansion, where he found the wife, still weeping.

"Your husband is in great danger," said Tom. "Robbers have captured him, and they threatened to kill him if he does not give them everything he possesses. He asked me to come and tell you and lent me his boots."

At this, the poor woman gave Tom a lot of treasure, which he stuffed down the magic boots, then made his way quickly to his parents' home.

Oh, what rejoicing there was! His brothers said they would go back and fetch the rest of the ogre's treasure, but first they all sat down and enjoyed a mighty feast.

And now, at last, Tom's family realised that though he was

only small, he was a very, very clever person indeed!

Of course, some people try to say that Tom Thumb never did take away the ogre's gold and treasure, and that he only took the magic boots to stop the ogre from chasing them any more.

They also say that after he tried on the boots and found they fitted him, he went straight to the king, who happened to be anxious for news of a battle his army were fighting in a far-off land. Thanks to the boots, they say, Tom Thumb was able to go for the news and bring it back, all in one day, which pleased the king very much.

But however it happened, Tom did become very rich, and neither he nor his family ever went hungry again.

The Snow Queen

THE SNOW QUEEN

A long time ago, in a far off country, there lived some very small people called gnomes, who did nothing all day long except play nasty, cruel tricks on other people.

One of them, who was very bad indeed, and very clever at thinking up cruel things to do, had made a magic mirror, which turned everything reflected in it into ugliness, and every person who looked in it into a bad person.

He had a lot of fun with this, going from town to town, holding it up and causing a lot of unhappiness wherever he went, which pleased him very much.

But one day he dropped the mirror by accident, and it broke into thousands and thousands of tiny pieces. And at that very moment a very strong wind blew up, which picked up all these pieces and carried them off, flinging them here, there and everywhere.

"Oh, splendid!" screamed the gnome, thinking of all the unhappiness this would cause.

But he wasn't glad for long. The same wind picked him up, too, carried him off and threw him down somewhere, so far away that from that day to this, no one ever heard of him again.

Now in the country where the magic mirror had broken there was a very large city. And in one of the poor back streets of this city were two houses, standing opposite each other. They were tall, thin, dirty, unhappy houses.

And yet in the attics of both these houses lived a family who was not at all unhappy.

Because in one of them lived a young boy called Danny, who was kind, playful, loving and intelligent. And in the other family in the opposite house lived a little girl called Gerda. Danny and Gerda were great friends, and spent a lot of time together.

They had decided long ago that the street where they lived was really very ugly, so they had done something about it, and built two little gardens, one on each of their balconies. Here they grew flowers, and plants in pots which climbed all over the walls, all round the windows and right up to the roofs. It all looked very pretty indeed, just like hanging gardens, a lot of people said, and it was lovely to see them in this neighbourhood, where there was no grass, no trees, nothing that was fresh and growing.

"Danny! Look! My forget-me-nots have opened, and my marigolds are beautiful!" Gerda would call across, happily.

And Danny would reply. "And I have some beautiful bluebells and geraniums and nasturtiums. I will give you some of their seeds."

So, despite their poor life, Danny and Gerda were both very happy, and it was their dearest wish that they should never be separated.

But the wicked gnome spoiled this wish, because the wind

that carried off him and his bits of broken mirror, passed over the town where the children lived, and three tiny pieces of mirror fell down and touched Danny's eyes and his heart.

The pieces of mirror were so tiny that Danny did not even feel them. He picked them up and looked at them with surprise, then threw them away and never thought of them again.

But in that moment, everything that had always looked so good and beautiful, now seemed ugly and silly and unbearable.

"Oh, these tiny gardens are stupid!" he cried. "And you are

just a silly girl, Gerda! I don't want to play with you any more! I'm off, into the town, to find some better fun!"

"Oh, Danny, Danny, please don't go away!" begged Gerda. And she began to weep.

But he just shrugged his shoulders and ran off, down the stairs four at a time till he reached the street, where he ran as quickly as he could towards the noisy, crowded streets of the town.

Gerda hoped he would come back, but days, weeks and months passed and she never saw him. Winter came, and the flowers in the little balcony garden where he had been so happy faded and died. But he never came to see them.

And, although Gerda never stopped thinking of him, Danny did not give her one single thought.

In fact, he had joined up with a gang of young rascals, and by now he was the worst behaved person in the town.

"There he is! That's him! Danny the thief . . . the cheat . . . the hooligan! He ought to be arrested and sent to prison!" people began to say, pointing at him in the streets.

But the police never could catch him, because he knew all the dark little corners in the twisted old streets. He knew how to get away and hide.

But that winter happened to be a very long, cold and hard one. A great thick blanket of snow covered the streets and it was almost impossible to walk along. But Danny stole a fine blue sledge from two young children who were playing in the snow, and from then on he was able to get around very easily, and go anywhere he wanted. It was great fun, rushing around in the stolen sledge.

Then one evening, when the cold was worse than it had ever been, Danny became lost, in a part of the town he had never seen before. Shivering, and very hungry, he searched around for somewhere to shelter for the night, when suddenly two beautiful, fine white horses came galloping along.

They were harnessed to a magnificent sledge, sprinkled all over with glittering stars, and inside it sat a pale lady dressed in thick, snow-white furs.

The horses stopped suddenly beside him. The lady spoke to him and told him to come and sit beside her. He did so, and immediately the horses went on at a great speed, through a terrible snow storm.

Danny began to tremble with fear, it was all so strange, but the lady just stared straight ahead of her, just as though she

were made of ice. Then Danny suddenly fell asleep, and as he did so, he forgot everything that had ever happened to him.

And still, during all this time, Gerda went on thinking about Danny. At last, when the winter was over and spring was near, she decided to go into the town and look for him.

She found the hooligans he had lived with and spoke to them, and they told her that the last time they saw him was during a fearful snow storm in the winter, when they also saw a fine sledge drawn by two white horses, travelling very fast towards the north. It was a very frightening night, they said. They thought Danny was in the sledge

So Gerda could find no trace of Danny, but as the weather grew warmer and flowers appeared, she resolved to go after him to the north.

She said good-bye to the old grandparents with whom she lived, and set off, alone and on foot.

Soon she arrived at a river, where a small boat moored to the bank seemed to be waiting for her. She stepped in and cast off, and just as though it knew where to go, it sailed off down the river. Past bright fields and pretty villages it went, sailing down the middle of the river.

After they had travelled a good distance, the boat drew in to the bank and stopped, right opposite a little thatched cottage. There was an old lady standing at the door, and as the boat stopped, she walked towards it.

"Welcome, dear child!" she called out, kindly. "You look very tired. Won't you come in and have some food and a rest?" And she led Gerda into her house.

As soon as Gerda had eaten something, the old lady said: "Dear me, how untidy your hair is! It is so pretty, too. Let me brush it and comb it. Just sit here and keep still."

She began to comb Gerda's long, fair hair with a golden comb, and as she combed, little by little Gerda began to forget all about her past life, and Danny, and the grand-parents she loved.

Because the golden comb, and the little boat, were magic things, and the kind old lady was a witch who was looking for someone to live with her and keep her company. So she had cast a spell on Gerda, and in only a few minutes the little girl did not wish to go away.

She stayed there for some time, because the old lady was not a wicked witch, and only made good magic. But then one day Gerda had gone outside for a walk, and she happened to notice the flowers which were blossoming in the garden of the little thatched cottage, and they were all the ones that Gerda and Danny had grown in their own little balcony gardens.

And at that moment Gerda remembered everything, and broke the witch's spell.

"Oh, Danny, Danny, my very best friend! How could I have forgotten you like this!" she thought.

She must go on searching for him. She must find him!

And when the old lady was not looking, she ran away towards a forest not far from the cottage.

She ran deep into the forest. It became dark, and she thought she could hear bears and wolves in the distance. But on and on she went, afraid that the witch might still find her, and did not stop till she came to a poor little wooden hut.

"Help! Help!" she cried, and knocked at the door.

It opened, and there stood a young country girl.

She wore very rough clothes, but she looked kind and took Gerda into the hut, and gave her some food. She told Gerda she lived there all alone, with a great reindeer for company, and a lot of birds, whose language she had learned.

Then Gerda told her story, and the country girl was so very sorry that she called some of her bird friends, who knew everything that happened, everywhere.

"Oh, yes, we can tell you about that," they said. "We saw a boy like that riding in the Snow Queen's sleigh one night last winter. She was going home to her castle at the North Pole after she had been away making that terrible snow storm. The boy was beside her, fast asleep."

"How can I find the North Pole?" asked Gerda.

"It begins just where there is a thicket of trees, covered in red berries all the year round."

"And can I walk to it?" asked Gerda.

But the country girl then spoke to her reindeer, and said she would set him free if he would take Gerda to the Snow Queen's castle. He promised to do this, and the next morning Gerda said good-bye to her new friend, climbed on to the reindeer's back, and off they galloped.

"Soon I shall see Danny again. Then I shall take him home

and everything will be just the way it was," she told herself, gripping the reindeer's neck.

It became very cold. Snow was falling in great flakes. At last the reindeer stopped by a thicket covered with red berries. This was as far as he could go. Gerda had to walk the rest of the way.

And so she entered the Snow Queen's kingdom.

But not once in all this time had Danny thought of Gerda. In fact, he had still forgotten everything, because not only had the wicked gnome's bits of mirror changed his heart, but he was also under the Snow Queen's spell.

So, without memory, without joy or happiness or any kind of

feeling, he lived in the Snow Queen's magnificent palace, which was made entirely of ice. But Danny cared nothing for the wonderful things around him. Even when he went for a walk and met the Snow Queen's charming baby bears, he was not a bit interested.

The days were very long and boring.

The Snow Queen was disappointed. She had taken Danny because she thought he would be a nice companion, and she didn't know why he wasn't happy. So one day she said to him: "In this cold country of mine, there are no gardens or green lawns, no trees or flowers of any kind, because nothing seems to grow here. But I would like very much to taste some of the wonderful fruits which grow and ripen in the countries of the South. I am going to travel there, and I shall load up my sleigh with strawberries and cherries, pineapples and pears and anything else I can find. There won't be room for you in the sleigh, Danny, so you will have to stay here till I get back. I shan't be long."

So there he was, all alone, but he didn't mind. Nothing mattered to him. He didn't even want to escape.

And there he was, still all alone, when Gerda arrived at the palace at last, after a terrible journey on foot through that bitter land.

She went into the palace, and saw Danny.

The poor girl was half dead with cold, hunger and tiredness.

The wind had torn her clothes, and she looked terrible.

"Oh, Danny, Danny, at last I have found you! Come home with me – come now, this minute! Let us get away from this dreadful place, back to our own homes, where we were so happy!"

Alas, he did not know her. He pushed her away from him.

"Who are you? Leave me alone and get out of here," he said.

When she heard these cruel words, she began to cry. After her long search, and her terrible journey, how dreadful to hear Danny telling her to go away, staring at her as if he did not know her.

But then he watched the tears rolling down her cheeks, and stared. Each one seemed to flow into his heart, softening it, till little by little he began to remember everything . . . .

"Gerda!" he cried suddenly. "Oh, Gerda, is it really you? What are we doing here in this dreadful place? Come, let us go. Let us go home."

He took her hand and they ran out together.

"Oh, Danny, so you do remember me, after all?" she panted, as they ran.

"Of course I remember you! I don't know what happened to me, or why I suddenly forgot you," he said.

And Danny never did find out about the wicked gnome's broken mirror, or realise that Gerda's tears had broken that evil spell.

On and on they ran across that icy land, until at last they came to the thicket of red berries.

And there, on the other side of the thicket, the kindly old reindeer was waiting for them. He had not gone away, after all, but had stayed there and waited for the gentle little girl whom he had brought to this dreadful country.

They both climbed on to his back and off he went, towards the warm, sunny south where they lived and had been so happy, and where their tiny balcony gardens were still waiting for them to plant new seeds and make the old street look beautiful again, as they had done before.

And as they galloped on, Gerda told Danny how she had made up her mind to find him, and the strange adventures she had had.

And Danny was so very sorry for all the trouble he had caused, and thought how good it was to see the sun shining in the sky, and to have such a wonderful friend as Gerda.

"I shall never go away again, Gerda," he said.

Happy Days at Flowerville

THE castle of Flowerville stood in the middle of a splendid park, in Normandy. Lady Flowerville, who was a widow, lived there all the time with her children – John and Tessa, Charlotte and Margaret, and little Sophie, an orphan child whom she had adopted.

In the summer, for the school holidays, she usually invited friends and relations to come and stay at the castle, together with their children.

How happy they all were!

The eldest cousin was called Lionel. Then there were Charles, Henry, James and little Arthur.

Of course the visitors wanted to see everything and do everything all at once, and Tessa and Charlotte were kept very busy making plans for outings and games and all kinds of amusements. The children could not bear a minute when nothing was happening.

When the weather was fine, they were able to go outdoors, but if it rained they had to stay inside.

But whether they were inside or out, they managed to have fun, and quite a few adventures, too.

THE WHITE LAMB

One day, the grown-ups decided to go off for a long walk through the woods. As it was a hard walk, they left the youngest children at home, and told Lionel he must stay, too, to look after them.

He was not at all pleased to miss the walk, and have to look after the little ones at home.

"Oh, this is too bad!" he grumbled. "Me, having to look after them! Just look at them, playing with that stupid toy lamb on wheels!"

He meant Sophie and Arthur, who were having a lovely time playing with the lamb. It was a very nice lamb indeed, covered with curly white wool. Its eyes were like blue forget-me-nots, and it had been a Christmas present.

They took no notice of Lionel's bad temper, but took it in turns pulling each other up and down on the white lamb.

Lionel watched them for a while, tossing a ball up and down.

He said suddenly. "Did you hear what I said? I said that lamb is silly and absurd. It's very common, too. Pooh – a white lamb! Now, if it had only been a black lamb, it might be worth looking at."

"But how can we change it from white to black?" they asked.

"You could paint it black, of course."

"But we have no black paint."

Then Lionel, who had only been teasing, had a very naughty idea. "You could use black ink," he said.

They didn't realise he was teasing. Arthur rushed off and fetched a bottle of black ink from his mother's room, forgetting he had been forbidden to touch ink.

Lionel knew he was being very unkind to the little ones, but still thought he should have been allowed to go with the others.

So he did nothing at all to stop Arthur, who took the lid off the bottle and emptied half the ink over the white lamb.

Little Sophie laughed and laughed. Arthur threw the rest of the ink over the lamb.

And what a terrible mess it made!

It splashed on to the walls, the curtains and the carpet. There were stains on the children's clothes, on their hands and faces – except Lionel, of course, who was careful to keep well away from it. He was still nice and clean.

"Oh, well done!" he cried. "You both look splendid now!"

But young as they were, Arthur and Sophie knew they did not look splendid. And when they looked round and saw the ink splashes everywhere, they began to feel very guilty.

Soon, all the others arrived back from their walk, and when they saw the two little ones and the mess they had made, Arthur's mother was very cross indeed with him.

She told him he could stay like that for the rest of the day, and he must go to bed without supper.

"I suppose you realise you look very, very silly," she said severely.

All the other children began to laugh at them, but now it was Lionel's turn to feel guilty. He was not really an unkind boy, so he confessed that he was really to blame for it, and asked Arthur's mother to forgive him.

And seeing that he really was sorry, she did forgive him.

THE MOUSE

"I can hear a funny noise from inside that cupboard," said little Sophie one day. "Ssh . . . can't anybody else hear it?"

Yes, there was a scratching noise. The children opened the cupboard, and there inside was a tiny hole.

"That's a mouse hole. A mouse must live in there, hiding away from the cat," said the children's nurse. "If you want to catch the mouse, you must put a trap there with a little piece of cheese in it."

So Charles and Henry went to the village and bought a mousetrap. Then they put a piece of cheese in it, and quietly closed the cupboard door.

"Now we must all be very quiet so that we won't frighten the mouse away," whispered Henry, as they waited.

"But . . . ."

"Ssh!"

After they had waited a long time, James quietly opened the door. "Oh, we've got it!" he cried. "There's a lovely little grey mouse inside the trap!"

"Oh, poor little thing – let it go," said Charlotte.

"Yes. It wants to go back to its nest," said Tessa.

"No. Let's have a good look at it," said Lionel. "We've never had a real live mouse before."

"Why don't we tie a long piece of ribbon round its neck so that it can't escape, and then we can let it out of its cage?" suggested Charles.

No sooner said than done. Tessa ran off and found a long

piece of blue ribbon.

They tied it round the mouse's neck, then put it on the floor. But the poor little thing was so terrified by the voices and movements of the children that it leapt off the floor and began to climb up Charles's leg.

"Help! Help!" he screeched.

But the others were frightened, and climbed on to the table away from the mouse. Their nurse came in then and laughed at them, and said they were babies.

Then they decided to take their mouse for a walk in the garden. But they hadn't gone very far before a large cat came creeping up, getting ready to pounce on the poor little thing. James chased the cat away.

"I really think our little mouse might be a lot happier on its own, without us. Shall we let it go?" asked Charlotte.

"Yes, yes!" they all agreed.

And they took the ribbon off the mouse, who scuttled away, delighted to be free again.

THE THIEF

Mark and Michael, who lived not far from the castle, were sometimes invited to come and play in the garden with the castle children.

One day while they were there, it began to rain, so Charlotte took them all to her room and showed them her photograph album, of which she was very proud.

Some days later she was again looking at her album, when she noticed that some pages had been cut out, and her best photographs were missing.

She was very upset about this. She didn't know who had done it, and she told her Uncle Frank, who was visiting at the castle.

He thought about it, then said: "Don't worry, Charlotte. I know a way to catch the thief. Now, I want you to invite everyone who was here that day, to come again to-morrow. Will you do that?"

Charlotte did this, and the next day they were all there again. Then Uncle Frank took them into the library, where he drew the curtains so that everything was dark, then put on the table a basket covered with a white cloth.

"This is a magic basket," he said. "If any-one who is a thief puts his hand into it, it gives a great roar."

Then he asked everyone to come to the table one by one and slip his hand very quietly under the cloth and into the basket.

They all did this. In the darkness, each one came forward, slid a hand into the basket, then went away without a word. It was all very mysterious.

But no roar came from the basket. Not even a tiny sound did it make.

Then Uncle Frank drew back the curtains very sharply. There stood all the children in a row, and to their amazement they saw that everyone's right hand was covered in flour ... everyone's, that is except Michael's!

But as they all looked at him, his face grew very red and guilty.

"I am afraid it was Michael who took the photographs," said Uncle Frank, sadly. "You see," he explained. "That is not a magic basket. But it is full of white flour. I knew that if the thief thought the basket would roar, he would not put his hand into it. So there would be no white flour on his hand. And I was right, you see. Everyone except Michael has white flour on his hand. So I say it was Michael."

Michael hung his head and nodded.

Lady Flowerville was very cross about this. She took Michael home, and told his parents what had happened. And she said that unless they punished him, she would not be able to invite him to the castle again.

As for the other children, they felt very unhappy to think that one of their friends could behave so meanly.

THE WHITE DOG

One fine sunny day the children were idling around the garden with nothing to do.

"What shall we play?" asked Arthur.

"Shall we have a sack race?"

"Oh, no, it's too hot!"

"Hide and seek?" suggested Margaret.

"No – that's just a girls' game," said Lionel, trying to be all grown up.

"Why don't you all take a walk in the woods?" suggested Lady Flowerville. "It's cool and shady there. You should enjoy that. But don't do any silly things, like getting lost."

This sounded very pleasant, so off they all went.

As Lady Flowerville had said, it was lovely in the woods,

cool and shady. They walked along, laughing, chattering, and finding plenty of fun.

They came to a clearing, and the girls and the little ones decided to sit down for a rest. But the boys had seen a great oak tree, and decided to climb it.

Charles reached the top first, and perched there on a great branch. "I wonder if we can see the castle?" he said, looking around.

He could not see the castle, but suddenly he cried out: "Well, really! There's a horseman over there on a path, and he is whipping a little white dog . . . oh, how cruel!"

"Let's go and see if we can find this man and make him stop it," said Henry.

They scrambled down to the ground, and followed by the other children, ran off to find the cruel horseman.

But when they reached the path, the dog had run away, and the horseman, red and angry, galloped past the children to try and catch it.

The children were very upset, and started to go home. But as soon as they left the wood, to their surprise the poor white dog crept out of a clump of bushes and came towards them, wagging his tail.

"He has followed us! He wants to come with us! Oh, Charlotte, do let us take him home," begged the others.

They arrived back at the castle. Charlotte told her mother what had happened, and asked if they could keep the dog. Lady Flowerville did not know who the cruel horseman was, but she agreed the dog could stay.

So he stayed. He was very friendly and affectionate, and the children loved him very much.

But one day they went to the woods again, taking the dog with them, and suddenly they met the cruel horseman. He recognised the dog, and told the children they must give him back. Immediately, he thrashed the dog soundly.

The children were very upset about all this, and never stopped talking of the dog. "Oh, I wonder what has happened to him?" they sighed. "Why does his master whip him so much, and treat him so cruelly?"

In the end Lady Flowerville went off and bought them a new puppy, black this time and very playful. They called him Frisky, and he was so happy and funny that the children loved him right from the start.

But one day, as they were all having breakfast, the door opened and in ran the little white dog, looking very excited to be back amongst his friends.

"Oh, poor dog! See how thin he is! He has been starved as well as whipped. Look, he has broken his chain to come back to us!"

The white dog came towards them . . . but then suddenly he saw Frisky the puppy, who yapped and tried to climb on to Henry's knee.

The white dog stopped, very still.

Then he gave a loud, unhappy whine, as though he felt that his friends had forgotten all about him. He turned and ran off quickly, before anyone could stop him.

They went after him to bring him back. They searched everywhere, but it was no use. He had vanished. They never saw him again.

But some time later Lady Flowerville found out who the cruel owner was, and she heard that the dog had gone back to him, but had died . . . of sorrow, one of the man's servants said.

The children were very grieved to hear this. They could not forget what a friendly and loving friend he had been.

SHRIMP FISHING

At the other side of the woods was a small waterfall which fell into a rocky pool, where fresh-water shrimps could be found. One day, as a special treat, Lady Flowerville took the children there.

After a splendid picnic they took off their shoes and stockings and went into the pool to catch shrimps. The boys had brought some small baskets. They put tiny pieces of meat into them, then sank the baskets into the pool.

"Now we all have to sit very still, and quiet, and wait for the shrimps to come into the baskets and eat the meat,"
said Lionel.

"Why do we have to sit still and make no noise?" asked Sophie.

Henry explained. 'So as not to frighten the shrimps away. This is an easy way of catching them."

But Sophie was not a little girl who could keep still and quiet. Soon she was wading into the water and splashing about. But suddenly –

"Help, help!" she cried.

James ran into the water, picked her up and carried her to the bank. "Something caught hold of my toe!" she wailed.

"I expect the shrimps have nipped you with their claws. You were told to be quiet and still, you silly thing," he said.

And all the children laughed at her. "Perhaps that will teach you to do as you are told," they said.

She was not hurt, and now she did keep quiet, and soon the boys brought in their baskets, and found some very fine large shrimps there. Tessa, who was always neat and tidy, arranged them in one of the baskets on a bed of fresh green ferns. "We shall cook them to-night for our supper," she said. "And they will turn as pink as – as – "

"As Sophie's big toe!" cried Margaret, laughing.

They all laughed, and went off to find Lady Flowerville, who was waiting for them.

But that was the last of their adventures for that summer, because the holidays were almost over, and all the children must start getting ready to go back to school.

It seemed very sad to say good-bye, for it had been such a wonderful summer, but it couldn't be helped.

The castle children stood at the gates and waved the visitors off.

"Come back next year!" they cried. "We've all had a lovely time. Have a good journey home! Good-bye, good-bye!"

And they watched till they were quite out of sight.

Donkey-Skin

THERE was once a very good, kind king, who believed that he was the happiest man in the world.

His people loved and respected him, and there was prosperity in his kingdom. He lived in peace with other kingdoms. The queen his wife was gentle and good, and their only daughter was the most beautiful and charming girl anyone had seen.

And that wasn't all. In his stables the king had a most unusual donkey. Every morning, amongst the donkey's straw, there appeared a large quantity of brand-new, gold pieces.

So, thanks to this magic donkey, the king had made a very large fortune, and so was able to live in great luxury with his wife and daughter. Of course, he was very fond of this donkey, and gave orders to his servants that he must always be well fed and cared for.

But then came a time when the queen fell ill, and did not get better. At last she knew she was going to die, so she said to the king: "My dear husband, our daughter is still very young. I am worried in case she marries someone who is more interested in her fortune than herself. Promise me you will only agree to let her marry someone who truly loves her, who in fact would die of sorrow if he could not marry her."

He was very upset, but he did promise his queen what she wished, and she died peacefully. Then the whole court, and all the people of the land, mourned for her.

But at the king's court there was one knight who was very sly and deceitful. He had overheard what the queen had said to the king before she died, and he began to plan how he could marry the young princess and so get hold of her large fortune.

First he asked the princess to marry him, but she refused with horror, for she did not like him. But then he took to his bed, and pretended to be very ill indeed, shivering all the time as though he had a great fever.

Hearing of his knight's illness, the king visited him.

"What is your trouble, my friend? What can we do for you? Where is your pain?"

"Sire, it is in my heart. You see, I love the princess, your daughter, and if I cannot marry her, I shall die of a broken heart. Oh, if only our dear queen were alive, I am sure she would understand how I feel, and make the princess marry me."

This, of course, reminded the king of his promise to the queen. "Cheer up, my friend," he said. "I promised the queen before she died that the only man I would have for a son-in-law is one who would die for love of my daughter. I shall tell my daughter that we need look no further than you for her husband . . . and we shall soon celebrate your wedding."

And he sent for the princess, told her she was to marry the knight and she must start preparing for the wedding.

This made the poor princess very unhappy indeed, and she was in tears.

But then she remembered her godmother, the fairy Lilac,

who had always told her to come and see her if she was in trouble. So off she went, in her favourite little carriage drawn by a white sheep. And when she arrived, she told the fairy Lilac all her troubles.

Lilac thought about it for a long time, then said: "I have an idea. Tell your father that you want a dress the colour of the weather, and will not be married till you have it. He will not be able to give you such a dress, for who can make the colour of the weather?"

The princess thanked her godmother, went back to her father, and said before she was married, she would like a splendid dress the colour of the weather.

The king was very surprised at this, but he wanted to please his daughter, so he sent for the finest designers and dress-makers in the kingdom, and told them they must do what the princess wished, no matter how much it cost. And if she was not pleased, he said, he would have to punish them.

So they all set to work, and three days later they came back with a marvellous dress which really was the colour of the weather, embroidered all over in beautiful soft shades which seemed to change all the time.

The poor princess was amazed at having been so quickly obeyed, and she didn't know what to say. So off she went again to see her godmother.

"Yes. They were a lot cleverer than I thought," said the fairy Lilac. "Very well. This time ask for a dress the colour of the moon. They will not do it, for the moon changes all the time."

The princess was overjoyed, thinking that now she would not have to marry the man she so disliked. She asked her father for a dress the colour of the moon.

Alas! Only two days later back came the clever dress-makers, and brought a dress so beautiful that it really did look like the moon.

It was so lovely that she had to pretend she was now satisfied.

But once more she visited her godmother. "Oh!" she wept. "What must I do, not to have to marry that man?"

"Ask your father for another dress – this time the colour of the sun. And they will fail, for who can imitate the colour of the sun?" cried the fairy Lilac. "Cheer up! We shall win, you'll see!"

But no. Once again the dressmakers came back to the palace, with a dress so marvellously embroidered with gold thread, and stitched all over with diamonds, that it sparkled and shone just like the sun.

In fact, the princess had never seen anything so splendid. And at last she had to agree to the wedding. But she was in such despair that she went to her room and stayed there, weeping. And this time, her fairy godmother came to her.

"Be brave, dear child. I have thought of one last thing. Ask your father to give you the skin of his priceless donkey to make a coat. He will refuse, of course, for everyone knows how precious the donkey is to him. I promise you will never have to marry this man whom you dislike."

But the fairy was wrong again, because when the princess asked, the king did not hesitate for one moment. He had his donkey killed, then brought the skin to her.

"Here is your coat," he said. "And now I am beginning to feel angry, for you are not behaving as a princess should. There can surely be nothing else you want, so your wedding will take place to-morrow. I have arranged it."

The princess was now desperate. The only thing she could now do was run away. And during that night, when everyone was asleep, she put on the donkey's skin, pulled it over her head, and daubed soot on her face to hide her beautiful pale skin.

It was a very black night. She had never been out alone like this before, and as she hurried through the forest, she was shaking with fear and cold.

All night long she walked, and when morning came she saw that she had walked right through the forest and was now near a small village.

A farmer's wife saw her pass and felt sorry for her. She looked so lonely and tired and unhappy, and very odd indeed, wearing that donkey skin coat.

So the woman called out. "Hullo there! Are you looking for work? I can give you a job, if you want it."

The princess was pleased, for she had no idea where to go. She said she would like to work on the farm.

But she looked so dirty and neglected, the woman did not take her into the house with the other servants, but gave her a little hut at the back of the farm.

And there she lived for many months, and no one knew except her fairy godmother.

But none of the other servants would have anything to do with her. They thought she was strange, because she always wore her coat pulled up over her head and her face was always dirty. They called her Donkey-Skin, and made fun of her, and gave her all the worst jobs to do.

But every evening when she had finished work, Donkey-Skin locked her door, lit her candle, then washed herself all over, brushed and combed her long golden hair, and put on some of her jewels and one of the wonderful dresses her father had given to her. Her fairy godmother had sent these things to her by waving her wand.

Dressed like this, the princess would then sit and dream of those happy days when her mother was alive. And sometimes she would wish that she could meet a handsome young man who would love her.

And she began to wonder how much longer she would have to go on like this, doing hard and dirty work, living in this poor hut.

But during the day time she just worked, and did everything she was told, and spoke to no one.

But the farmer's wife was a kind-hearted woman, and she could see that her new servant was a gentle and obedient girl and very hard working. She felt a little sorry for her, so one day she said:

"Donkey-Skin, you work very hard and I think you must be tired. Just for a change, you can take the geese and the turkeys down to the wood so that they can peck around there. It will be a little rest for you. But be sure to get back here before it is dark, because I shall need you."

So Donkey-Skin took the geese and the turkeys into the wood, and was pleased to sit down and rest, though she took some spinning with her to pass away the time.

After she had been there for some hours, she heard the sound of a horn, which she guessed was being blown by some hunter who was lost in the woods. So she called in the geese and turkeys and drove them back to the farm, for she did not wish to be seen. She knew people laughed at her because of the way she looked, and she had become very shy about this.

She did a few jobs for her mistress, then returned to her little hut.

And as usual she lit her candle, washed herself all over, put on her jewels and one of her dresses. She chose the Sun-dress, this evening. But then as she sat there, she began to wonder about the hunter in the woods.

"Who was he?" she thought. "An old and greedy man like that evil knight who has driven me from my home? Or could it have been someone young and kind and handsome?"

And she sighed to herself.

But in fact, the hunter she was thinking about was actually the son of the queen of a neighbouring kingdom.

He had gone out hunting in the forest which he did not know very well, and towards the evening he had become lost.

He had been sounding his horn to attract the attention of anyone who might be around, but no one appeared to have heard him, and now he found himself on a path, and he could see a tiny light at the end of it. He went towards it, and saw it came from under the door of a shabby little wooden hut.

He could hear nothing from inside the hut. Nor from anywhere else around him. He bent down, and looked through the key hole of the door.

And he saw an amazing thing! There, in that miserable place only big enough to store tools, stood the most beautiful young girl he had ever seen!

And she was wearing a dress that shone and sparkled exactly like – the sun!

He stared for several minutes. Then he knew he had to speak to this girl, so stood up and knocked at the door.

Immediately, the light went out. He knocked again, and called out, but – nothing. Only silence and darkness.

After a while he went away, along the same path, and came to the farm, where the farmer's wife invited him in and gave him food and drink. She told him exactly where he was and how he could get home.

But when he asked the woman, and the other people there, who was the beautiful girl he had seen in the hut, they all began to laugh.

"Beautiful girl! You are mistaken, Sir. The only person in that hut is our maid of all work who does our odd jobs, and she's no beautiful girl! She's dirty and plain and always wears a coat made from the skin of a donkey. In fact that's her name – Donkey-Skin!"

He just couldn't understand it. He went back to his mother's palace. But he just could not forget the girl he had seen, who looked just like the sun . . . so beautiful, with her long shining hair, and her sparkling dress.

And he didn't believe he had dreamed it, yet they had told him at the farm there was no such person. It began to worry him very much.

Soon he became very ill. He could no longer study. He neglected his royal duties. His mother, the queen, was so worried that she thought he was going to die.

"My dear son, what ails you?" she asked. "What can we do for you to make you well? Is there anything you want? If you will only tell us, you know we will bring it, no matter what it is."

But by now he hardly knew what he was saying.

"I want a cake baked by Donkey-Skin," he said. "She lives in the hut. Donkey-Skin must bake me a cake."

The queen did not understand this, and feared he had lost his mind. But just the same she sent out her servants to enquire, and they soon found that there really was a girl called Donkey-Skin, who lived in a broken down hut.

They spoke to her and told her their prince was dying, and asked her to make a cake for him.

Then she realised it must have been the prince who had knocked at her door one evening, when she had been wearing her Sun-dress. Had he seen her, she wondered?

She locked herself into the hut and baked a fine cake, full of all kinds of good things. But she happened to be wearing one of her rings, and while she was mixing the cake, it slipped from her finger and fell into the bowl.

And when the prince came to eat the cake, he found the ring. He looked at it and said: "This ring is so small it could only have been worn by a very small hand. Find this girl for me, and I know I shall get better. I shall marry her, whoever she is, and no other."

The queen then summoned all the girls from her kingdom to come to the palace, but the ring would not fit any of them.

Then a girl wearing a coat made from a donkey's skin appeared, and everyone gasped, for she looked so poor and neglected. But she held out her hand to try on the ring, and it slipped quite easily on to her middle finger.

Then she flung off her coat, and there beneath it she wore the dazzling Sun-dress which the prince had seen before.

And suddenly, the fairy Lilac appeared before them, and while everyone gasped with surprise, she waved her wand – and there stood the old king, the princess's father!

How happy he was to find his beloved daughter again! And how gladly he consented to her marrying the prince, for, he said, you truly did almost die of love for her.

The Story Of A Donkey

I am a little grey donkey, born on a farm somewhere in Normandy, France.

Everyone says I am very pretty, clever, bright and mischievous. Well, that may be so, but I was not at all happy at that farm, because my mistress the farmer's wife, was a large, cruel woman who ill-treated me very much.

She never stopped tormenting me. She never missed a chance to beat me with a stick, and she didn't give me enough to eat. I used to sob when she came near me to make her see how unhappy I was. "Hee-haw! Hee-haw!" But it made no difference. She just went on being cruel. She had no kindness in her.

Tuesday was always the worst day of the week, because that was the day she went to market to sell her farm produce.

As soon as it was daylight, she would fill huge baskets with masses of vegetables, fruit, butter, eggs, cheese, chickens, geese, ducks and rabbits. Then she loaded these baskets on to my back ... and climbed on top of them!

Oh, what a weight! Sometimes I kicked to try and get rid of some of it, but down would come her stick and she would shout: "Stop that and get along, you lazy thing! Hurry up, we're going to be late!"

And when we arrived, she would unload her baskets, tie me up in a corner, and without giving me anything to eat or drink, go off to a cafe to meet her friends and refresh herself.

But one day, she was in too much of a hurry. She left one of her baskets just where I could reach it.

I kept looking at that basket. I was hungry and thirsty, as usual.

I stretched out and helped myself to a tender, juicy lettuce. It was delicious!

So I took another. Then a fine cabbage. Then some crunchy carrots. Lettuce – cabbage – carrots .. I just went on and on eating.

What a feast! I had never enjoyed myself so much. It made up for some of those long miserable days when she hadn't given me anything at all.

Before I realised it, that basket was empty, and I was looking at another one, wondering if I could reach it . . . . .

When suddenly I heard her screaming, and there she was running towards me, furious, waving her arms above her head.

"Oh, you thief of a donkey! You wicked beast! See what he's done? I'll make you pay for this!" she screamed, and set about me with her stick.

Oh, how she beat me! I was sore all over, but then, suddenly, I became very angry. With all my strength, I kicked with my back legs – three or four times, I remember.

And there she was, rolling about on the ground.

A great crowd had gathered. They helped her up, smoothed her down and sympathised with her.

But nobody sympathised with me. They took no notice of me at all. They didn't even see that I was tugging hard at my rope.

Suddenly, it broke! I was free! I broke into a gallop and made off as fast as I could.

She saw me then. "Stop him! Stop him!" she screamed. "Somebody catch him and bring him back!"

She chased after me, followed by a crowd of her market friends, all shouting and waving their arms.

I tried to keep very calm. I ran through the market as fast as I could – upsetting a lot of things as I passed them, I am sorry to say – then I reached the streets and galloped at top speed, going down little back alleys which twisted and turned.

I was looking for somewhere to hide, so that I could lose my mistress and her friends. And at last I found a dark corner and hid there.

I could still hear their voices, quite near me. Then my mistress said:

"Well, he doesn't seem to be anywhere about. I expect he's gone back to the farm."

And then – they went away. I had lost them!

After a while I came out and quietly trotted off into the country-side. I came to a little wood. It wasn't far from my village, but there were plenty of places for me to hide. And there was fresh grass and roots and water I could feed on.

So I stayed there a while, till the weather became cold and very wet. Things had stopped growing, and I could find very little to eat. I was getting hungry again.

I could see that if I stayed there, I would die of cold and hunger. So I left my pleasant little wood and trotted off. I took care to keep going away from my village. And I thought how nice it would be if I could find a new mistress or master who would be kind to me.

Suddenly I saw ahead of me a beautiful little castle, surrounded by a large garden. Some children were playing in the garden. They looked kind and happy.

I went up to them and put my head on a little boy's shoulder, then a little girl's shoulder.

This surprised them, but they stroked my neck, then took me to their grandmother.

"Grandmother, look at this lovely little grey donkey. He just came up to us. May we keep him?"

The grandmother looked at me. "You can – as long as he doesn't already have a master," she said.

When I heard this, I shook my head very hard, trying to say "No, no, no." "Well!" said the grandmother. "He seems very intelligent. He seems to know what I said! But I will send the gardener out to-morrow to ask around and see if anyone has lost a donkey. If not, we will keep him. It will be very nice for you to have a donkey. Give him something to eat . . . and make sure you treat him well."

Hurray!" cried the children. "And we'll call him Bobby."

Well, no one ever did find out where I came from, because the castle was a long way from my cruel mistress's farm. So there I stayed, and was very happy indeed with my new masters, who were all kind to me, and acted as though they loved me.

I enjoyed playing with the children, and we had quite a number of adventures.

There was a little cottage not far from my stable, where a lady and gentleman and their little girl Pauline lived. Pauline often saw me and talked to me, and I had become very friendly with her.

But one night, when everyone was asleep, I woke up in my stable to a strong smell of smoke, and saw great flames shooting in through the window.

But the door was locked, and I was tied to the wall by a strong rope. I could not escape. I was terrified. I began to bray as hard as I could.

"Hee-haw! Hee-haw! Hee-haw!" I shouted.

I was almost in despair, when suddenly the stable door was pulled open, and there was little Pauline. She ran to me, untied my rope and tried to guide me outside – but by now there was fire all around us, and Pauline fell to the ground, overcome by the smoke.

Quickly I bent over her, took a great chunk of her clothing in my teeth and managed to lift her and carry her out of the stable. Her clothes had started to smoke, but there was a horse trough nearby full of water, and I dropped her in it.

She recovered, I am glad to say, and had no burns.

Some time later, something else happened.

One of my best friends was Bruce, the gardener's dog. We were often together and got on very well. But this happiness was not to last.

There was a boy living nearby who sometimes came to play with John and Tessa at the castle. His name was Peter and he was not a nice boy. He was always boasting, and playing nasty tricks, and trying to show off.

He often boasted that he could shoot very well, but no one believed him, so one day he secretly borrowed his father's gun and brought it to the castle. "Watch me shoot that pigeon in that tree!" he said.

Bang! went the gun, but he didn't shoot the pigeon; instead the bullet went straight through poor Bruce's heart, and he died immediately.

Everyone was very upset, but that didn't stop Peter from coming again.

One afternoon in summer the children took me for a walk in the woods, and we stopped by a pool where there were a lot of green frogs. Peter was there, too, and I decided to play a trick on him. I picked up a frog in my mouth, then gently slipped it into Peter's pocket.

Presently he put his hand into his pocket for his handkerchief ... and felt something cold and soft there, moving about. He gave a wild yell, nearly jumped out of his skin, and when the children laughed at him, ran off, shouting rude things.

I laughed at him, too, and brayed after him.

One day the children's grandmother organised a donkey ride into the country, and she hired several more donkeys from the village. John, the eldest boy, was riding me, and we were quite a large company – his sister Tessa, and Pauline, Elizabeth, Charlotte and her sister Margaret, and the boys, Charles, Henry and the awful Peter.

Everything went very well at first. John and I were leading the way and the others followed us. But presently we came to a wide stream with a wooden bridge across it, and as I looked along the bridge, I noticed that some of the planks in the middle looked rotten, and unsafe.

I stopped, and refused to take another step.

"Come on, Bobby, why have you stopped?" asked John, stroking my neck. But I did not move.

"He's just a stupid, scared donkey, that's why!" shouted Peter, who didn't like me much.

"No, he isn't. If he doesn't want to cross the bridge, he has a good reason for it," answered John.

"Oh, ridiculous! Well, I'll show you how to treat a stubborn animal like him!" cried Peter, boastful as ever.

And he whipped his own donkey with the stick he was carrying. The donkey, suddenly frightened, rushed galloping at the bridge and crossed it. But when he reached the middle, we heard a loud cr-r-rack! And the planks gave way.

Down went Peter and the donkey, straight into the water below.

"Help! Help! I can't swim! I'm drowning!" screamed Peter, splashing around in the water.

Just then I noticed a pole leaning against the arch of the bridge. I took it between my teeth and dragged it to the boys. They understood what I meant, and pushed it out to the middle of the stream, so that Peter could grasp it. Then all the children heaved and pulled, and were able to bring him in to the bank.

Streaming with water, crying and miserable, Peter went off home to change his clothes. "Good riddance," I said to myself.

After he had gone, we carried on with our ride, and about mid-day came to the ruins of an old abbey.

"We ought to leave the donkeys here to rest under the trees. We'll take our picnic and go into the wood and find a spring," said Charlotte, who was a very sensible girl.

And after they had tied us to the trees, they went off, carrying their picnic baskets, and we donkeys were left alone.

But scarcely were the children out of sight, when I saw some bad looking men come creeping out of the cellars of the ruined abbey. They looked all round, and when they were sure there was no one about, they began to talk together.

And from their talk I knew that they were planning to steal us, hide us in the abbey cellars till it was dark, then take us away during the night and sell us on some market.

Sure enough, they began untying us, and would you believe it, all the other donkeys just trotted off with them, nice and quiet, instead of braying as loudly as they could and trying to stop them.

It made me feel wild! I wasn't going to be stolen, just like that!

So I started the loudest commotion I could, braying at the top of my voice. "Hee-haw! Hee-haw! Hee-haw!"

And when they came towards me to untie my rope, I lashed out with my back legs. Wham! Bang! Crash!

And the men were rolling all over the ground!

Not one of them could get near me!

Well, of course they didn't like all this noise and bother. So in the end they left me alone, still tied to the tree, but took all the other donkeys away and led them into the abbey cellars.

And soon, everything was still and quiet again.

But at their picnic spot in the woods, the children had heard me braying. They all came running back.

How surprised they were to find only me, and not a sign of all the other donkeys. "They haven't broken loose," said Charles, puzzled. "There isn't even a bit of rope left behind."

"Well come on, let's start searching for them," said John. He untied me and began to lead me. "You help, too, Bobby. Where are they?"

In and out of the ruins they all went, and after a while they came to the door of the cellars. But I did not feel happy about it, thinking of those bad men. They had looked very dangerous. They might even have guns. I thought I must not let the children open that door and go in there.

So I stepped in front of the door and would not let them come near.

"I think he is trying to stop us from going in there," said Tessa. "We ought to go home and tell grandmother."

This was just what I wanted. I nodded my head very hard, in the direction of the castle.

"Look – Bobby's telling us to go home!" cried Charlotte. "So let's go!"

They put the two smallest children on my back, and off we went back to the castle, taking the shortest way we could find.

As soon as we arrived, the children told their grandmother what had happened, and she immediately sent for the police.

When they arrived, the police chief said to her: "As a matter of fact, there have been a lot of robberies in this district lately, and we haven't been able to find the thieves. These may be the people who stole your donkeys. I must say your donkey Bobby seems very intelligent. He was quite right to stop the children going into those cellars."

The grandmother patted my neck and smiled at me.

He went on. "My men and I will go to the ruined abbey and look around. I would like to take Bobby with us. I think he may be useful to us."

So, an hour later, we arrived back at the ruins, but of course there was no one to be seen.

So I went to the cellar door, lifted up my head and brayed, very loudly. I tried to sound very sad and unhappy, as though I were calling to the other donkeys.

It was a terrible noise I made.

And after a while the cellar door opened and a couple of men poked their heads out, to see what was going on. Then the policemen rushed at them, and took them by surprise.

In no time at all they were all handcuffed and being marched away. The other donkeys were brought out, and then we all went home together.

Oh, what a fuss everyone made of me! I felt quite proud of myself. Especially a few days later, when the grandmother arranged a village fete – with me as the guest of honour!

Everyone came, of course. They all stroked and patted me and kissed me, and gave me a great bundle of thistles, which I enjoyed very much, because thistles are my favourite food.

More Holidays at Flowerville

ANOTHER summer had come, and school was over. The children of Flowerville were looking forward to the holidays very much, because once again their cousins and friends were coming to stay at the castle.

This year, Lady Flowerville had also invited an old friend of hers to visit them. Mrs. Rosberg was not a happy lady. Her husband, who was the captain of a ship, had been lost at sea. Everyone hoped she would enjoy being with all the children, and join in their plans.

On the day they were to arrive, no one could keep still. From early morning little Sophie kept running down to the gates, keeping a lookout for them.

But at last they arrived, and what happy greetings there were!

"Lionel, how you've grown since last year! And you're thirteen now!" cried Tessa, looking at her cousin.

"Charles too! And just look at Henry, he's almost a young man and he's only seven," said Charlotte.

"Well, we've got all kinds of plans for you," said John. "Walks in the woods, picnics, and a lot of new games. . . ."

"Yes, you're going to have a lovely time, but now we must take you to your rooms and let you unpack, then you can have a meal. You must be hungry," said Lady Flowerville.

For the next few days the weather was lovely, and the children played in the gardens, chasing butterflies with their nets, looking up favourite places in the woods.

They gathered lots of blackberries and wild strawberries and mushrooms.

In the evenings, before they went to bed, Lady Flowerville and Mrs. Rosberg told them stories.

The weather became warmer. One very hot day they went into the orchard, where there was a stream, usually full of fish. Some of the boys had brought their fishing rods, thinking they would catch some fish.

After an hour or so of fishing, John's basket was full, but Lionel hadn't caught anything. This put him into a bad temper and he couldn't stop grumbling.

"Oh, it's much too hot! I don't like it here. Can't we find some more shade? Isn't there a summer hut where we can shelter from the sun?"

"We've often tried to build one, but we don't seem to be able to make it stay up," said Charlotte. "It's a harder job than you think."

"But we built one in our garden at home, and that's still standing. Isn't it, Charles? We'll build one for you."

Seven-year old Henry clapped his hands. "What a good idea! I'll build one, too, for Sophie and Margaret and me."

Lionel scoffed at his cousin. "Don't make me laugh, Henry! A little boy like you can't build a hut."

"I can, too!" shouted Henry. "I shall start to-morrow and Sophie and Margaret will help me, then you'll see!"

That evening the children went into two groups, secretly making their plans for building the huts. Lionel and Charles drew shapes on a piece of paper and Lionel kept laughing at Henry and the two little girls, whispering together at the other side of the room.

But what a surprise the older boys got when they went out next day to start their hut! The younger children were already there working on their hut, which was looking very well.

Lionel seemed so annoyed at this, that Henry and Sophie and Margaret now laughed at him. But Charles said:

"Goodness, Henry, how have you managed to do so much at it already?"

"Well, Sophie and Margaret and I got up very, very early this morning and we've worked hard since then. In fact we're so tired now that we're going for a rest. Work hard, you two!"

Charles and Lionel did work hard, but they had great trouble making the supports for their hut stay up. They just couldn't get it right. And yet there was the little ones' hut, almost half finished already.

It was the same the next day. And yet . . . they didn't actually see the little ones working. They always went off for a rest as soon as Charles and Lionel turned up.

"There's something very strange here," said Lionel. "I just don't understand it. Charles, I think we'll get up at dawn to-morrow and come out here to watch the children working."

And so they did . . . . and lo and behold! They saw Henry's father, who was spending a day or two at the castle, working on the hut!

Henry's father laughed. "Yes, Lionel," he said. "I'm the one who built the hut for them. You see, you kept on making fun of them – but they're a lot younger than you."

Lionel looked ashamed. "Yes, I did. I'm very sorry, uncle. I promise I won't do it again."

And after that all went well. Henry's father helped Lionel and Charles, as well as the little ones, and soon they had two splendid little summer huts. The whole family went to look at them, and said they were lovely and very useful.

Some days later, the children invited the grown-ups to go into the wood and have a game of hide and seek. It was decided that the children should hide and the grown-ups should find them, but everyone was forbidden to climb trees.

All went well for a time and they had great fun, but then Lady Flowerville noticed that she hadn't seen little Sophie for a while.

"She must be lost!" she said. "Now then everyone – we'll all keep together and look around and keep calling her."

They did this, and called loudly, but there was no answer from Sophie.

Now they became really worried, so they broke up into groups, with a grown up in charge of each, and made a bigger search.

Suddenly, John heard a faint cry. It came from the inside of a tree! "Help! Help! I can't breathe! I shall die!"

"Did you hear that?" gasped John, to Mrs. Rosberg. "This tree is hollow and Sophie is inside it! I shall have to climb it."

He had to climb quite a way up before he found the place where Sophie had fallen in, and then he couldn't reach her. But he took off his shirt, twisted it into a rope and let it down, then managed to drag Sophie up.

She was very frightened, and glad to be rescued, and very sorry to have been so disobedient and climbed the tree.

But she was safe and sound, thank goodness, She was very grateful to John, and told Lady Flowerville that she would never disobey again.

It was soon forgotten, and everyone was happy again, except Mrs. Rosberg, who could not forget about her shipwrecked husband.

Sometimes she would go and visit a lady called Mrs. Lamont who lived not far from the castle, and was the wife of one of the sailors who had been on Captain Rosberg's ship. He also was lost.

Then one day, as the children were walking in the woods, they saw a tramp, sitting on a log. He looked tired and weary, but spoke to them, and asked them if he was going in the right direction for the village. His wife lived there, he said, and her name was Mrs. Lamont.

The children realised that this was one of the people who had disappeared with Captain Rosberg's ship!

They showed him a short cut to the village, then ran home and told Mrs. Rosberg. Right away she went off to see him, and to learn what had happened to her husband.

"When the ship was wrecked," said the sailor. "Only three people stayed alive. Captain Rosberg, a young boy called Paul, and myself. We got ashore to an island. But there were natives on the island, and they captured us. I managed to get away, but Captain Rosberg and the boy Paul didn't."

"I did my best to rescue them," he went on sadly. "But I couldn't. I have no idea what happened to them, but I am afraid they are dead. I had to keep in hiding as much as possible, and I thought I would die, too. But one day a boat came and they took me off, half dead with starvation. They were kind to me, and put me on a ship going to Le Havre. I've walked all the way here from there."

Mrs. Rosberg wept at this, but she was very glad the sailor had been saved, and went often to visit him and talk about her husband.

But alas, there was no news of Captain Rosberg and the boy Paul . . . . until one evening when Mrs. Rosberg was walking in the garden, and saw two people entering the gates.

And one of them was her husband, the captain!

Oh, how happy they were to see each other again!

The other person was Paul, a fine looking boy of twelve, and the children were all happy to meet him.

Soon he was telling them of his adventures. His parents had been drowned in the shipwreck, but Captain Rosberg had managed to save Paul and had looked after him ever since.

And he said the captain had become friendly with the natives on the island, who had treated them kindly, until at last they

had been found by a ship that called at the island for water, and had been brought home.

And now, Captain and Mrs. Rosberg had decided to adopt Paul as their own son, as he was now all alone.

He was happy at Flowerville and was soon like one of the family. He, too, built a little summer hut, near the other two, and they looked very neat, all in a row.

Lionel, who was not at all brave, began to admire Paul very much and liked him a lot. He made up his mind that in future he would try and be like Paul. But of course, that was not easy.

They were out walking one day when they heard shouts of bullying laughter, and some crying and pleading.

"Someone is in trouble! Let's see if we can help," said Paul. But Lionel hung back.

"Don't you think it might be dangerous?" he asked.

"What does that matter, if someone is in trouble?" said Paul, and he dragged Lionel along.

Round the corner they found several hooligans who were tormenting a little lame boy. Paul sprang at them, and Lionel did the same.

They snatched the little lame boy away then tackled the hooligans and gave them such a hiding that they ran off.

Then they quietened the little boy, gave him some sweets, and sent him off home.

"You see, it is easy to help your neighbour, Lionel," said Paul.

Yes, Lionel did see. He decided that in future he would try to be braver and kinder, especially to younger children.

But alas, the holidays came to an end, and the visitors had to get ready to leave. Some were going to Paris, some to Lyons, and Paul, of course, was going to his new home with Captain and Mrs. Rosberg.

It was another sad parting, but they all promised to write to each other often, and tell all their news.

After the children had waved them off till they were out of sight, they went back indoors and sat talking about all the exciting things that had happened.

Building the huts – losing Sophie and then finding her – and most especially the return of the sailor Lamont, and Captain Rosberg and Paul.

It had been one of their best holidays.

Goldilocks and the Three Bears

ONCE upon a time there was a very pretty little girl, whose hair was so long and golden that everyone called her Goldilocks.

She lived with her parents in a nice little house, not far from a large forest.

She liked living there. She liked the great trees which smelled so delicious, and the little stream that flowed through the garden. But she had no brothers or sisters and there were no other children nearby to play with, so sometimes she felt lonely.

She was very curious about the forest. It seemed so mysterious. She would have liked to go in there and have a look round, but her mother always said: "No, Goldilocks, you must never go further than our gate. There might be wolves in the forest."

This made her shiver, but it didn't stop her from being curious. And one day, she slipped out and went into the forest.

It was certainly mysterious, but very interesting, with the sun shining through the tops of the tall trees, and making strange shadows.

She found lots of flowers of all colours. Then she saw some lovely mushrooms, all bright yellow and brown. She was just going to pick one when a rabbit watching her near-by called out: "Don't touch those, Goldilocks! They are poisonous and will make you very ill."

She could hardly believe the rabbit had spoken, but she said: "Oh, thank you, rabbit. I won't touch them."

Then a squirrel called out: "Hello, little girl, it's nice to see you. Why don't you come and see us more often?"

But then a wise old owl said: "No, no. Go home, Goldilocks. It is not very safe for you in the forest alone. You might get lost, or you might fall down and get hurt."

This frightened Goldilocks, and she ran away as fast as possible. But then she saw a little path, and a lovely thatched cottage right at the end of it.

It looked very bright so she went closer. She forgot to be frightened and was curious again. Also, she felt a little tired. So she went to the door and knocked. No one answered, so she opened it and went in.

She was in a very cosy room, all very nice and neat. But all was still and silent. She walked around, looking at things. There was a lovely old clock in a corner that she liked. She stood in front of it and wished it could talk.

Then she noticed a large table, covered with a bright checked cloth. On it stood three bowls, each full of delicious looking porridge.

She realised that she was not only tired, but very hungry, too, and the porridge seemed to be waiting to be eaten.

She tried to pick up the first bowl, but it was too heavy. So she tried the porridge with a spoon, but it was too hot.

So she tried the next bowl, but that was too salty.

Now she really was hungry, seeing all this food here. She tried the next bowl.

It was smaller than the others and she could lift it up. She tasted it. The porridge was not hot. It was not salty. It was just right.

She ate it all up!

"That was a very nice breakfast," she told herself, and went on exploring the little house.

She came to a pleasant sitting room, where she saw three armchairs, all different sizes, each one with a pretty cushion.

"I'll just sit down," she thought. But when she tried the largest chair, it was too high for her to climb on to it.

She tried the next one, which had a spotted cushion that she liked.

But it wasn't a comfortable chair, and she soon left it.

The smallest chair looked to be just the right size for her. "I'll sit on that," she thought. She ran to it and sat down with such a bump that the chair broke under her weight.

Oh, dear! She tried to put the pieces together again, but it didn't seem to be right, so she left it.

And as she turned away, she noticed a small staircase against the opposite wall.

Ah, that looked interesting! She went up the stairs, and they led into a very pretty room, decorated in blue. There was a portrait of a bear on top of a chest of drawers.

She opened the drawers, and found a lot of lovely silk scarves, all in different colours. She liked those very much indeed.

She tried a few of them on, admiring herself in the mirror. But then she noticed three beds, all in a row, covered with soft eiderdowns.

Oh, how tired she was! She went to the first bed and tried to climb on to it, but it was too high.

She tried the second bed, but it was too hard.

Then she tried the third bed. This was just the right height, and very comfortable indeed.

"I'll just rest here awhile," she said, and fell asleep.

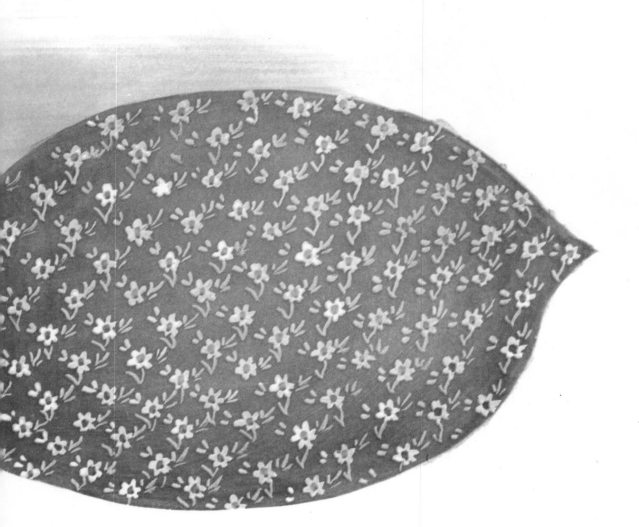

Now this pretty little cottage in the middle of the forest belonged to a family of bears.

There was Mr. Bear who was very proud and strong and clever. He had made all the furniture that was in the little cottage.

Then there was Mrs. Bear. She was very clever too, at sewing and embroidering and housekeeping. She had made all those pretty scarves which Goldilocks had tried on. She liked scarves, and wore a different one every day.

Last of all was Baby Bear, a mischievous little chap, who gave his mother a lot of trouble with his games and tricks.

This morning they had made their usual breakfast of porridge, then gone out to get some things they wanted while it was cooling.

Now they were on their way home, carrying their parcels, while Baby Bear chased the butterflies that fluttered all around.

Catching butterflies was not easy. Baby Bear was a little put out, the way they flew away from him.

But soon they arrived at the cottage. Suddenly, Baby Bear cried: "Oh, look, our door is open! Someone must have been inside."

They all looked at each other. Then they went in. Everything was very quiet.

But ... just look at that untidy table! "Someone has moved my bowl!" boomed Mr. Bear, in an awful voice.

"Mine, too! And someone has been eating my porridge!" twittered Mrs. Bear. "Oh, really, who can have done this dreadful thing?"

But then Baby Bear gave a loud screech. "Oh, oh, oh! There's only a spoonful of porridge left in my bowl! Someone has eaten it all up!"

This was really terrible! Big tears came into Baby Bear's eyes and ran down his velvety nose.

His parents tried to cheer him up.

"There, there, little one, don't cry! We shall find whoever has done this awful thing and he will be punished for it."

"And I shall make you some more porridge, very creamy and sweet, just the way you like it," said his mother.

But Baby Bear couldn't stop crying. Oh, what a bad morning it had been! He had found nothing interesting on their walk. He hadn't been able to catch one single butterfly, although he had run after them so very hard.

And now, when he was so tired, and so hungry, there was no porridge!

It was too bad.

They began to search around. Under the sideboard, behind the clock, under the table. Nothing at all! And everything so quiet and still.

"Let us go into the sitting room. Perhaps we shall find something there," said Mrs. Bear, rather timidly, for she was beginning to feel frightened.

"Yes, we'll do that. Everybody into the sitting room," said Mr. Bear, sounding very brave.

But when they reached the door of the sitting room, they did all keep close together . . . and they just poked the tips of their noses round the door.

Then they groaned.

"They've been in here, too! They've moved my armchair and crumpled my cushion!" said Mr. Bear.

"My cushion is on the floor and the chair has been knocked over," said Mother Bear.

Baby Bear screamed.

"Look at my chair! It's all broken up into little pieces!"

"What cheek! Coming into our house and doing things like this!" said Mr. Bear.

"We will go upstairs," he said. "And see what we find up there. Keep very close together."

One behind the other, they crept up the stairs towards the bedroom, trying

to make no noise, because they were all a bit frightened now. They wondered if some sort of monster had got into the house.

In the bedroom, everything was untidy again. Things were thrown about. Mrs. Bear's pretty scarves were lying around. The drawers of the chest were open.

"What a terrible mess!" growled Mr. Bear. "And someone's pulled my eiderdown to the floor!"

"And my pillow is all crumpled!" said Mrs Bear.

But then Baby Bear screamed. "Come over here, quickly! Look, I have found the monster – asleep in my bed!"

They all rushed over.

154

And there lay Goldilocks, fast asleep in Baby Bear's bed!

"But it isn't a monster! It's just a little girl, with beautiful golden hair!" they said.

All this time Goldilocks had been fast asleep, and dreaming that she had changed into a fairy with lovely wings, and lived in the forest. Under a huge mushroom, an orchestra of rabbits was playing lovely music.

Everything was happy and gay, and she was enjoying it all very much.

Suddenly the dream vanished. She woke up.

Baby Bear's voice had wakened her. And what a fright she had, seeing three bears leaning over her!

She screamed, leapt out of bed, ran down the stairs and out of the cottage.

They called after. "Oh, don't run away, little girl! We shan't harm you. Stay a little while."

But Goldilocks didn't hear them. She was already far away, running as fast as she could.

She didn't stop running till she arrived home, and flung herself into her mother's arms.

Oh, she would never disobey again!